Maddi's Fridge

Written
by
Lois Brandt

Illustrated
by
Vin Vogel

Flash
Light PRESS

For Mom and Pop. —LB

For Michael. —VV

ISBN 9781947277762 (8x8 paperback)
ISBN 9781936261291 (hardcover)
ISBN 9781936261383 (EPUB)
Library of Congress Control Number: 2013957177
Editor: Shari Dash Greenspan
Graphic Design: The Virtual Paintbrush
This book is typeset in Schnitzle. The title is Fontesque Bold.
The art was created using a digital tablet and pen.
Flashlight Press · 527 Empire Blvd. · Brooklyn, NY 11225
www.FlashlightPress.com   Distributed by IPG

When Sofia and Maddi played at the park, they stretched their toes to the sky. They climbed to the top of the ladder and flew off the end of the slide. They stayed until the buildings grew long shadows and even the taxis stopped honking.

"Let's play on the climbing wall," Maddi said.

"No way," Sofia said. "I can't reach."

"Yes way!" Maddi scooted up to the top of the wall. "Your turn!"

Sofia put a foot on the bottom rock, grabbed with one hand and stre-e-e-e-etched — but she couldn't reach the next hold.

Sofia's stomach growled. "I give up. Let's get a snack."

"No way," Maddi said. "Let's stay here."

"Yes way!" Sofia ran to Maddi's building...

...and raced up the stairs.

"Wait!" Maddi ran after her.

Maddi was the best climber, but Sofia was the fastest runner.

Sofia swung open the door of Maddi's fridge. "What have you got?"

"We have milk," Maddi said. "I'm saving it for Ryan. He's still little."

"Why doesn't your mom go to the store?" Sofia asked.

"We don't have enough money."

"But what if you get hungry?"

"We have some bread," Maddi said.

"I guess I'll go home to eat," Sofia said.

"Please don't tell anyone," Maddi said.

"Okay."

"Promise?"

"I promise."

Sofia ran home past the bookstore and grocery store.

The sun went down behind the buildings and took all the colors with it.

"Good timing," Mom said. "Dinner's almost ready."

Luis was wrestling on the floor with Pepito. Sofia opened the refrigerator door. Pepito peeked inside.

Sofia's fridge was full of milk and eggs and tortillas and cheese and lettuce and jam and salsa and tofu and even half a can of dog food.

"Here you go," Mom said.

Sofia and Luis each had a plate of fish and rice. Mom had a plate of fish and rice. Even Pepito had his bowl of dog food (with a little bit of fish and rice).

Maddi and Ryan only had some bread and a small carton of milk.

Sofia couldn't tell Mom. She had to keep her promise to Maddi.

"Not fish again," Luis said. "I want Cheesy Pizza Bombs."

"Cheesy Pizza Bombs are a treat," Mom said. "Fish is a good source of protein."

"Is fish good for kids?" Sofia asked.

"Yes," Mom smiled. "Fish is perfect for kids."

That night, Sofia had an idea.

"Yuck!" Maddi said the next day.

"Oh!" Sofia said. "Double yuck."

Fish may be good for kids,
but fish is not good for backpacks.

After school, Sofia and Maddi raced to the climbing wall.

Sofia got there first, but Maddi
scrambled past her to the top of the wall.
Sofia stre-e-e-e-etched
and stre-e-e-e-etched.

"Keep trying," Maddi said.
"You'll get it."

"I can't." Sofia jumped down.
"It's too high."

That night, Sofia, Luis, and Mom ate frittata. Pepito had his dog food (with a little bit of frittata).

Maddi and Ryan still had an empty refrigerator.

Sofia couldn't ask for help. That would break her promise. She had to try again.

"Are eggs good for kids?" Sofia asked.

"Not as good as Cheesy Pizza Bombs," Luis said.

"Cheesy Pizza Bombs are a treat," Mom said. "Eggs are good for you."

After dinner, Sofia packed eggs for Maddi and Ryan.

"Yuck!" Maddi said.

"Double yuck!" Sofia said.

Eggs may be good for kids, but eggs are not good for backpacks.

Sofia and Maddi raced to the climbing wall.

Sofia won again, but Maddi shot past her to the top of the wall.

Sofia grabbed one hold, re-e-e-e-eached for the next...

...and
came
down
with
a
thump.

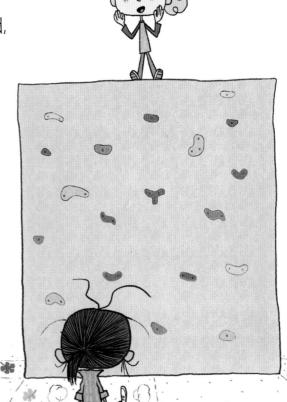

"That happens sometimes," Maddi called.

"This is impossible," Sofia said.

"Keep trying," Maddi said. "You'll get it."

That night Sofia, Luis, and Mom had burritos. Pepito had his dog food (with a little bit of burrito and no salsa).

Maddi and Ryan still had an empty fridge.

Sofia wished she hadn't promised Maddi.

"Are burritos good for kids?" Sofia asked.

"Burritos are very good for you," Mom said.

"Not as good as —" Luis started to say.

"You should pay attention to nutrition like your sister," Mom said.

The next morning, Sofia put two burritos in her backpack along with tortillas, beans, cheese, and even some milk.

"Um, no thanks," Maddi said.

"You haven't even looked!" Sofia said.

"Is it fish?" Maddi asked.

"No."

"Is it eggs?"

"No."

"Is it gross?"

"I don't know," Sofia said.

Maddi shook the backpack. Something sloshed.

"Let's look together," Maddi said.

"One, two, three –

GO!"

Burritos are good for kids, and good for backpacks too

"Do you want some milk?" Sofia asked.

"Thanks," Maddi said, "but I'll save the milk for Ryan."

Sofia and Maddi raced to the climbing wall.

Sofia won as usual, and tried to climb.

"You can do it," Maddi said. "Take my hand."

"Woo-hoo! I made it to the top!" Sofia shouted.

"We're the tallest kids in the park!" Maddi said.

"Thanks for helping me, Maddi. I couldn't do it alone."

Maddi shrugged. "That's what friends are for."

After they finished playing, Sofia walked home past the bookstore and the grocery store.

Her own fridge was full of milk and juice and chicken and yogurt and bread and carrots and even half a can of dog food.

She thought and thought and thought.

Maddi's fridge
only had
two tortillas
and
a cup of beans
and
a bit of cheese
and
a little more milk
than before.

Sofia didn't want to break her promise,
but she couldn't help Maddi alone.

Sofia told.

She hoped Maddi wouldn't be mad.

"I'm glad you told me," Mom said. "Let's see what we can do together."

They loaded grocery bags with milk, flour, chicken, carrots, sugar, oil, and even frozen meat and vegetables.

Luis pulled his package of Cheesy Pizza Bombs out of the freezer. He thought and thought and thought some more. Then he put his Cheesy Pizza Bombs in Maddi and Ryan's bag.

"For a treat," he said.

At Maddi's apartment, the moms talked.
Luis and Ryan played.

Sofia and Maddi ran to the park.

"You broke your promise," Maddi said.

"I'm sorry," Sofia said. "Are you mad?"

"A promise is important," Maddi said.

"You're more important," Sofia said. "I wanted you to have milk too."

Maddi smiled.

"Are we still friends?" Sofia asked.

"Always," Maddi said.

"Double always," Sofia said.

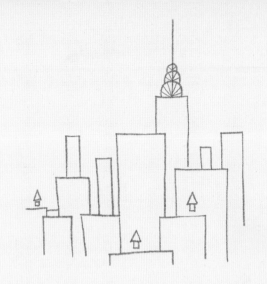

"Cheesy Pizza Bombs!" Luis yelled.
"Our moms made Cheesy Pizza Bombs —
for a treat!"

Sofia and Maddi raced up the stairs.
Sofia slowed down...
so they could run together.

That's what friends are for.

Let's Help Friends Who Have Empty Refrigerators

✔ Do you have a friend or classmate who never eats breakfast and doesn't bring food for snack at school? Tell a parent or trusted adult.

✔ When you have friends over to play, offer some fruit and a glass of milk. You can even make them Cheesy Pizza Bombs! (Go to MaddisFridge.com for the recipe.)

✔ Make posters encouraging people to give food or money to your local food bank. Ask permission to put your posters up in grocery stores, libraries, schools, and businesses.

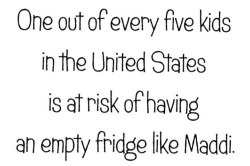

One out of every five kids
in the United States
is at risk of having
an empty fridge like Maddi.

✔ Volunteer with your family or class at a local food bank, pantry, shelter, or community kitchen.

✔ Ask your local food bank what foods they need. Then organize a neighborhood or school food drive for those items. (Your little brother or sister's wagon is perfect for collecting donated food.)

✔ Talk to your friends, teachers, and parents about ways to fight childhood hunger. The more we talk about empty refrigerators, the fewer there will be.

For links to hunger organizations and for more information about how you can help, visit www.MaddisFridge.com